MY DONKEY

AND

THE MASTER

A Short Story of
Sanctified Imagination

J.L. Callison

Cover photo by Malcom Brook

ISBN 978-0-9987771-1-5

EBook ISBN 978-0-998777-10-8

J.L. Callison
407 Hinman St
Aurora IL 60505

www.jlcallison.com

Dedication

To the Rev. and Mrs. David Crymble Jr., my father-and mother-in-law, who love me as their own, and from whom I received my wife. I shall be grateful to them forever for their acceptance, their love, their care, and their encouragement.

Acknowledgement

My long-suffering wife, Linda, has worked closely with me to edit this tale and make it readable. I am most grateful for the way she puts up with me—sometimes an unenviable task.

Table of Contents

MY DONKEY AND THE MASTER

The dust on the narrow dirt road puffs up around my feet as I walk. My burro stirs dust with each step as he follows behind on my lead rope.

I glance into the face of the woman riding the burro. She is exhausted by the events of the last two months. My wife walks alongside, to assist if needed.

I have known the lady now for over thirty years, from before she was married. I pondered how it all started.

****

Joseph Ben-Jacob* had been my father's friend, and they worked together building Sepphoris, Herod Antipas' city. My father, Simon bar Jesse, walked the hour and a half trek from Nazareth with Joseph every morning and then back each evening. Though Joseph was now a young man of only nineteen years, he and my father worked well together, and my father thought highly of him.

The day after I completed my Bar Mitzvah at age thirteen, as was our custom, Joseph knocked on our door at mid-day. "I have bad news," he said, face ashen. "There was an accident at work. The hoist rope broke and dropped a sling full of stones. Simon never knew what hit him. I'm so sorry."

At the end of the week of mourning, Joseph came to the house and called for me. "It is time now for you to take the

1

responsibilities of a man. As your father did for me, I will do for you. You'll be my apprentice until you are ready to take over your father's business. I will meet you here before first-light in the morning."

It is sad, but the only things my father was able to leave to me were his tools—and old Jed, his donkey.

Our three-hour trek to and from the job site each day allowed us plenty of time to talk and become fast friends. The age difference did not come between us any more than it had between Joseph and my father. We spoke of our dreams and ambitions, of our hopes and goals.

My burro plodded along carrying our tools.

****

One morning a year later, Joseph wasn't acting himself. All the way to work he had a smile on his face, and he hummed. Normally cheerful, today he was downright giddy. No matter how much I asked, he wouldn't tell me what was going on. It wasn't until the end of the day that I got the story. Joseph was in a hurry, and he kept trying to hustle my burro along faster than old Jed liked to travel. "What is your hurry, Joseph? Slow down, and take your time! It's been a long day already."

"Ah, my friend, I cannot slow down!" Even after a long day working in the heat, he still had that crazy smile on his face.

"Tell me, Joseph, what's the hurry? You've been acting funny all day long!"

Joseph looked around to be sure nobody was listening, although we were the only ones on the road at that time of evening. "Do you know Mary Bat-Heli?"

"Certainly, although not well. What about her?"

2

"My father and I are going over to meet with Heli tonight and ask for her hand in marriage. I've been so afraid someone would beat me to her, but tonight is the night!"

I tugged on old Jed's lead rope myself. "Why didn't you tell me, my friend? That is wonderful news!"

It was that night when they signed the Ketubah*, in the Shiddukhin ceremony*, that Joseph's life changed totally. All men's lives change when they take a wife, but in Joseph's case it was more pronounced than he had any idea! God had plans for him that he had no way of knowing—and certainly not of understanding.

****

Even though they were legally married with the signing of the Ketubah, Joseph did not take Mary with him and live with her. The terms of the Ketubah gave him up to seven years to build her a home—actually an addition on his father Jacob's house—and to save five hundred shekels* to give to Heli as the bride price. He had to also be able to show he would be able to support Mary properly.

Joseph worked hard for the next four years and saved every mite* he could scrounge. I helped him build his home every chance I could get, for I knew he would do so for me when my time came. If all went well, he hoped to claim her just before Passover.

About a fortnight after we set the last block in his wall, Joseph came from his house, head hanging. "Mary has gone to Judea to see her cousin, Elisabeth. I guess the cousin is with child, even though she's getting older. The whole family is excited, and Mary just had to go and visit for a few months. I'm not sure if she wanted to go, or if Heli just wanted to keep us apart until we marry."

I clapped him on the back and laughed at him, and we started on our way to Sepphora. "Cheer up, Joseph. It's not like you get to see her alone anyway. You've been complaining about that for how long now? You're getting there. It won't be long until you can claim her."

Joseph shook his head, and we trudged on to work. He really had it bad! For a guy who hardly even knew the girl, one look was all it took, and he was head over heels for her. Sure, she was a cute girl and all that, but seriously!

****

The next three months were filled with hard work, both in Sepphora and on Joseph's house. Old Jed proved his worth many times over as he carried stones for the house, but he was getting old.

"Jed, you're a blessing," I told him as I gave him a rubdown. "Your muzzle is gray now, and you are working too hard for a donkey of your age." He just nudged at my pocket, asking for the apple I had there for him.

Reuben Ben-Simon had a likely jenny* that he was willing to breed for only ten shekels, so I took him up on the offer. I knew Jed would be good yet for another couple of years, and about that time his foal should be ready to start carrying the load. Jed's thirty-five now, which is not terribly old for a donkey, but he's worked hard, and I think it's time to start taking it a little easier on him.

The end of the three months brought a celebration for Joseph and me, for we finished off his house, and he moved in. Joseph roasted a lamb for his parents and invited me and my mother over to celebrate with them. It was a lot of fun that evening, singing and dancing the hora around a bonfire of aromatic cedar. Now he only had to finish saving up the rest of the dowry, and he could claim Mary, maybe before Passover after all!

Next day, I hurt my foot when a stone rolled under me, and I ended up riding Jed home rather than walking. It wouldn't have been so bad, but I was not going to be able to go to synagogue the next day, on the Sabbath. The rabbi was teaching from the writings of Isaiah about the Mashiach*, and I always loved to hear of the Blessed One. Oh, how I hoped he would come to us in my lifetime! Anyway, I had to stay home and keep my foot elevated. I told Joseph he was to take Jed with him the next day when he went to Sepphora, with hopes I could make it the following day.

Joseph woke me early the first day of the week when he came to pick up old Jed, so excited he could hardly talk! "Oh, but you missed it yesterday at synagogue! Old Heli told us what Mary said, and the rabbi said it sounds like the forerunner of the Mashiach was born! Mary got home Friday from her cousin's home and told Heli what happened. She said her cousin Elisabeth— she's married to a priest who burns incense in the temple, and he had seen an angel who told him that Elisabeth would have a son, but they were to name him 'John' instead of after someone in the family, and Heli said Zecharias—that's Elisabeth's husband—doubted the angel at first, so the angel struck him dumb and said he would not be able to speak until after the boy was born."

"Hey! Slow down," I laughed. "You are talking on top of yourself and not making sense. I can't follow what you are saying."

Joseph shrugged, but he didn't slow down much. "Zecharias couldn't speak until he wrote, 'He shall be called John,' when his new son was circumcised. Mary told Heli that Zecharias told them everything the angel had said to him—that

5

his son was to be a blessing to many and that he was to prepare the way for the Mashiach!"

Joseph fairly danced about the room with excitement! At first I thought he was going to stay around and talk, but finally he went out and got old Jed and started down the path to Sepphora, singing as he went. I looked down at my foot, totally disgusted with myself for hurting it so that I could not have been at synagogue to hear this for myself!

****

What a change can happen in just a day's time! Yesterday, Joseph was singing on his way to work, as excited as he could be about the news of the Mashiach's possible forerunner and Mary being home, but today when he came from his house he looked like his closest friend had died, but I know he didn't— because I'm still telling the story!

Joseph wouldn't speak, but he raised a hand in greeting before turning and walking down the path without waiting to see if I followed. His head was bowed, whether in grief or thought I knew not. When I tried to speak, he just shook his head and waved a hand at me to say, "Leave me alone," so I did. It was a long silent walk to Sepphora that day, with nary a word coming from him. I don't think he even said anything while working. He moved about in a daze, so distracted he was nearly knocked over the wall by a hoist full of stone. Had I not grabbed him, I think he would have gone over. He didn't even acknowledge me for saving him, and he ignored the foreman who shouted at him to be careful. All he did was rub his shoulder where the stone hit and walk back to where he had been working.

Come lunch time he didn't eat. He opened his sack, looked in, and then closed it up again and sat, head in hands. He would not look at anyone or speak but just sat. I had to shoo away a few who tried to get him to talk, saying that he had something important on his mind, that he did not need to be disturbed; but I was worried.

I took a short nap, as normal during the heat of the day, but when I awoke to go back to work, I saw Joseph sitting with his face buried in his hands. I shook his shoulder, and he got up and walked to the ladder, stumbling once on the way. When there, he climbed, and we went back to work on the wall, still silent. I knew not what had happened, but obviously, it was something terrible!

At the end of day, when the horn blew, I had to remind him to gather up his cloak and bag before going home. Still he did not speak until we had walked more than halfway, nearly forty-five minutes. Finally he lifted his head, took a deep breath, and exhaled with a whoosh before looking across the burro at me.

"I'm sorry I've been in such a mood all day." He took another deep breath and sighed. "Heli came to my home last night with bad news. He returned my down payment on the dowry." Again, Joseph drew in a shuddering breath. "Mary is three months pregnant, and no, it isn't mine. I've been trying all day to decide what to do, and I slept not a wink last night for thinking of it. I don't want to make this harder for her than it already will be, so I've just decided to give Heli the bill of divorcement quietly, rather than take it to the council. He will accept it with no trouble, I know. There's no need to cause the family grief for something she did." His head dropped to his chest again, and for the first time I saw tears drop to his tunic. He said nothing the rest of the walk home.

"Aleichem Shalom*, my friend," I said as we arrived at home. Joseph nodded, mute.

I put Jed into the stable and threw hay in the manger before going in to fix supper. I then lay abed on my pallet for the longest time before sleep would come. Joseph and his problems had my own mind in a turmoil that I could not shake off. I knew he was hurting, and I found it hard to believe that Mary would cheat on him, but the facts spoke for themselves.

Next morn, I woke and got ready for work, though bleary-eyed and tired. When I got old Jed from his stall and loaded him for the trip to Sepphora, Joseph came from his house rubbing his eyes. He shook his head as if to clear it and then sat down on a rock next to the stable. "I'm not going to work with you today. I must speak with Heli, and if he will let me, with Mary." Joseph shook his head again as if to shake it loose. "I don't understand what's going on. Last night while I slept, an angel came and told me, 'Joseph, son of David, don't be afraid to take Mary to be your wife. That which is conceived in her is of the Holy Ghost. She will give birth to a son, and you are to name him Yahushua, for he will save his people from their sins.'" He rubbed his eyes.

"I've got to talk with them. I . . . I don't know what's going on!" Shaking his head again, Joseph turned and stumbled off, heading across town toward Heli's home. I had nothing else to do but to go on to work without him.

I'm not really sure how much work I got done that day. Joseph's words rang in my ears all day long. Could this be the Mashiach of whom he spoke? We have been looking for him for so many years, but surely the Mashiach wouldn't come to our little town. He is the one who will re-establish the throne of David! Why would a king come from a little backwater town like Nazareth? As I trudged home wearily, I finally settled my mind that Joseph had just had a dream. I mean, after all, look at the stress he was under. Why would an angel come to him? It had to have been just a dream!

Needless to say, when I finally got home after that long walk—it seemed so much longer without Joseph to talk with—

I was amazed to see Joseph, with Mary, Heli, and her mother, moving her few possessions into Joseph's home.

"Shalom Aleichim!" Joseph called, waving. "Join us for dinner, and share in our joy!" I waved and led old Jed into his stall and cared for him before dashing into my home to clean up and dress for dinner. From their garb it appeared to be a festive occasion.

As soon as I walked in Joseph's door, he embraced me and kissed me on the cheeks enthusiastically. His demeanor was so different from when I left him behind this morning.

Mary stood slightly behind him, with downcast eyes, waiting for Joseph to share their news. Heli and his wife stood across the room with Joseph's mother and father, looking a bit uncomfortable with the situation. Joseph handed me a cup of wine and insisted I be seated at the place of honor at his table. "We've waited for you to return so we could tell you! You won't believe what is going on! Mary, please, you tell him what you saw. I've already told him of my side of things."

Mary sat with head bowed, looking up only with her eyes, embarrassed at the situation. In a low voice, she told of the angel Gabriel appearing to her. "He said my son would be the son of God, that he would be given the throne of David. He is also the one who told me of my cousin Elisabeth, who had been barren but was in her sixth month. He said that was to show me God's word never fails to come true! I went to see Elisabeth, and I was there when her son John was born. Zecharias, John's father, had been struck dumb for over nine months, after the angel told him John would be born, and I was there when God gave him his voice back." She looked at Joseph and bowed her head again. "I'm so thankful to God for telling Joseph what has happened and that he was willing to believe. I know most won't, but Joseph said you will," she half-whispered. Mary lifted her head and looked me in the eye.

"I know it doesn't look right,   but I ask you to believe. I know Joseph counts on you because most others won't. It's going to be hard on Mother and Father, but they believe me now, too."

"The blessings of God be upon you and Joseph, Mary. I will always be here for you." Mary bowed her head in thanks, and we began the meal together.

Heli handed me bread for the sop, saying, "I'm grateful to you for understanding. We decided today the chuppah and feast would not be appropriate under the circumstances. In fact, Joseph allowed, as things stand, he didn't think anyone else would participate in the feast other than you, so this is our feast for Joseph and Mary."

"I'm sorry that I came empty-handed. I didn't think this night would ever happen. I ask your forgiveness, Mary." I was quite embarrassed by my oversight.

"No forgiveness is needed. You being here for us is all the gift I could ever ask."

We talked long into the night, enjoying what was to be one of the few happy celebrations the family would enjoy. We cannot question God as to why He does what He does, but it seems His servants always pay a great price to serve Him.

From that day, although Joseph took Mary into his home as his wife, they slept separately until after the child was born. Joseph, always high in my regard, was greatly elevated in my estimation.

****

The next few months went much the same as they had gone, with the exception that Joseph was always in a hurry to get home and see Mary at the end of the day. We still walked together to work and back. Things came to a halt about four months later though. A decree from Caesar proclaiming a census, and with it a tax, required all go to the city or village of our birth to be registered. The time was getting close for Mary to give birth, and by rights, she should not be traveling all the way to Bethlehem, but Augustus did not give any leeway for medical conditions or pregnancies. They had to go, like it or not.

The distance was about seventy miles if we were to go directly there. I say "we," because I'm a Bethlehemite, too. There is no chance we would go the direct way, though. To go directly would require us to go through Samaria, and no Jew worth his salt would go through Samaria if he could avoid it. The longer way required an extra twenty miles down the Jezreel valley to the Jordan and across, then down to Jericho and up to Jerusalem, then over to Bethlehem.

Normally one would expect to be able to make twenty miles a day, but with Mary's condition being what it was, we didn't figure to make more than about fourteen, which meant we had to find places to stay at night along the road. Usually, this would not be a problem because people would open their homes to travelers who needed a place to stay. However, since people didn't know the true story of Mary's pregnancy, nobody would take us into their homes. Joseph and Mary had not gone through the chuppah ceremony and feast, so they were still considered espoused rather than married, and thus people considered them to be living in sin.

So, we had to camp out along the way. I bought Reuben's jenny, Delilah, from him before we left because we had decided to remain in Bethlehem rather than return to Nazareth. The work on Sepphora was nearing an end, so we would soon be out of work anyway, and Herod was expanding work on the temple in Jerusalem. Joseph and I knew we could get hired there if we but showed up. With the jenny along with us to carry some of the lighter load, we had old Jed to give Mary a ride at least part of the time.

Mary was exceedingly uncomfortable by the time we reached Bethlehem. My uncle welcomed me in, glad to see me, but unfortunately for Joseph and Mary, the same was not true for them. Joseph was forced to seek shelter in the khan*, but alas, a caravan was in town, and there was no room. The owner of the khan allowed them to stay in the hay of the stable, along with others who could not get a room, as was customary.

I've often spent the night in a haymow when traveling, or even in a haystack out in the field if no other shelter was nearby. It isn't as bad as it might sound, as it is as soft as a straw tick, and if you burrow into the hay, it can be quite warm on a chilly night.

It is a good thing we arrived when we did because the travel caused Mary to go into labor, and she gave birth the very night we arrived. Neither she nor Joseph were quite prepared, so all they had for the child, Yahushua, was some cloth with which she wrapped him, swaddling him tightly, and she laid him in an unused manger until Joseph could see about finding a house to rent or buy. I didn't find out about all of this until later, when Joseph told me all that had happened overnight.

Half a dozen shepherds showed up at the khan before dawn, saying they had been out in the fields with the flock of sheep—kept for the Passover celebration—when an angel woke them up and told them of the birth of the Mashiach and described the place where they would find him. The shepherds said the whole sky was filled with angels praising God! Even though the angel told them not to be afraid, they were terrified, and just as soon as the angels were gone, the shepherds left their sheep behind and hustled into Bethlehem to see the child.

Next day Joseph and I found the publican*—a pox on him and his ilk—and registered for the census, paid our taxes, and then found a house he could rent for his family. It didn't take much to move their goods over to the house and get them settled. I returned to my family's home and spent a couple of days with them before Joseph and I went to Jerusalem to seek work at the temple.

****

Joseph and I enjoyed the next year and a half working on the temple. To us it was a special treat to work on God's house rather than rebuilding a very secular city for a tetrarch who had no use for God. It was nice to be able to work and worship at the same time.

Watching Yahushua grow was a treat for me. I had no brothers or sisters, so for me to be around a small child was a new experience. Joseph and Mary welcomed me into their home as if I was a brother, rather than just a friend, and I spent as much time with them as I could.

One day, Joseph and I had a particularly trying day, working through a rain storm that did not want to quit. Most of the men had been sent home, but our area had to be finished before the Shabbat*, and that left no time for quitting early. Needless to say, our feet dragged on the way home, both of us soaked and wanting nothing more than something to eat and bed.

Imagine our surprise when we turned into the lane that led to Joseph's home and saw a number of richly appointed camels gathered before his house. Several servants and camel boys sat against the wall, passing the time away as servants will when not at work. Joseph's steps quickened, and we hastened as much as our exhausted legs would carry us.

"Come in the house with me. You may as well eat with us before going home. No need for you finding something to eat on your own tonight. Besides, you might be interested in who this is and what they want, too."

I nodded my thanks and tied Jed to a picket stake where he could crop at some thin grass to hold him over until I could get him home and feed him properly. Joseph and I walked into his home to find several magi from Persia gathered around Mary and little Yahushua, praising God and blessing him. When Joseph and I entered, all stood. Balthazar introduced himself and the others saying, "We saw the star of the King of Israel in the east, and we have come to worship him. He was foretold by Daniel the seer, lo these many years ago, and we magi have watched for his star for over five hundred years—the very star that led us to your home."

Joseph looked at Mary questioningly, only to see her gentle smile in return.

"You are most welcome, of course, to our humble home. We did not expect you, but we are honored by your presence."

"Nay, but it is we who are honored! For us to have been allowed to see the Mashiach of whom Daniel spoke is a blessing for which we shall strive to be worthy. We bless your home."

Balthazar turned to a servant standing in the corner and spoke quickly in a foreign tongue I knew not. The servant scurried outside, and moments later he, followed by several others, returned to the room carrying small chests and bags, which they in turn gave over to Balthazar and the other magi.

"Please allow us to offer this small token of our esteem." Each of the magi knelt in front of Mary, who held little Yahushua, and placed their packages at her feet. As each man placed his gift before them, he bowed himself low and kissed the foot of Yahushua before stepping back. Joseph stared from one man to another with wonder in his eyes, while I was struck speechless!

One by one, the magi bowed to Joseph and walked out the door. They set up camp around the house for the night. In the morning, they would return to Jerusalem in order to report to Herod Antipas where they had found the Mashiach, as Herod had requested. He had said that he, too, wanted to worship.

I ate a quick supper with Joseph and Mary, and we discussed and wondered about what we had seen and heard. I then took Jed and went home in awe of what had happened. It took me quite some time before I was able to go to sleep.

Next morning, as I prepared for work, Balthazar told Joseph of a dream each of the magi had during the night in which God told them not to return to Jerusalem—or to Herod—but to return home a different way. Each of the magi gave their goodbyes and mounted up to leave.

I met them as I made my way over to Joseph's house and was saluted by Balthazar as they went past. Such finery I have never seen as was on those camels! It is a good thing they had such a large retinue of servants, else they would have been quite a prize for some of the brigands that lurked in the hills.

****

On the way to Jerusalem, Joseph and I discussed the meaning of the dream the magi shared. Why would they not go back to Herod as they had promised? What could possibly be wrong with telling him where to find the child so that he could come and worship also? That's what Herod said he wanted to do.

Neither of us could come up with a good answer, nor did we think there could be any danger to the child. Nevertheless, we both had a lot on our minds as we worked throughout the day.

After the long day and evening of the day before, we were weary as we trudged home. "Have you come up with any

15

J.L. Callison

ideas, my friend? Why would God warn the magi to hurry home a different way?" Joseph asked.

"I'm sure I don't know, Joseph. All I can say is, God's ways are not our ways. Did He not tell Moses to do things that made no sense at the time? God has his reasons, and they are always right."

"You have that right! Oh well. Goodnight. I'll see you in the morning."

We parted, and I cared for Jed. For some reason that I didn't understand, I added grain to his hay, and I gave a scoop to Delilah, the jenny I bought from Reuben, and to Ruth, her colt. Ruth was getting old enough that I had started breaking her to carry a pack. She nuzzled my pockets looking for the treats I usually had for them, and I gave her one while scratching her ears. Jed and Delilah were good animals, and faithful, but Ruth was special to me, and she knew it. She always nudged me until I gave her something each evening and always stood waiting for me to scratch her ears and stroke her neck. Perhaps our close relationship is why she was so easy to break to a pack, unlike other donkeys I have broken and trained for people.

I went into my house with a sense of foreboding hanging over my head, a feeling of dread that was totally unlike me. Normally I take things as they come, placidly, and I don't worry about the future. I never saw much sense in worry. After all, what could it change? Still, I couldn't shake the feeling.

I ate supper and went to bed, exhausted, but sleep was a long time coming. When it finally came, it was fitful, leaving me unrested.

****

It was not yet dawn when I heard loud knocking. Struggling to awaken, I stumbled to the door.

16

"Who is it?"

"Joseph. We need to talk. May I come in?"

"Certainly! Come ahead." I opened the door wide and gestured for Joseph to enter and then lit a lamp so we could see.

"An angel just came to me in a dream and told me to take Mary and Yahushua to Egypt—that Herod will try to kill him. Would you sell me Delilah? I need something to carry all of our goods, and Yahushua is not able to walk all that much yet."

I looked at Joseph and could see how urgently he needed to go. "No, I won't sell her to you. If you can wait just long enough for me to throw my things together and get ready, we'll all go together."

"That's too much. I can't ask you to leave everything and go with me."

"You didn't ask. Besides, if Herod's men come looking for me to find out where you are—if I'm not here they can't ask me—now can they? You would be sitting ducks for bandits if you went alone. I'll go along, and between the two of us we can protect Mary and the baby."

"Thank you." Joseph lowered his head. "That is much more than I could ask for, but you will be a big help, especially if you take all three of your burros along. Thank you, my friend."

We both hurried out to my little stable and threw some grain out for the animals, knowing they would eat it more quickly than hay, and it would give them more energy for the road. Perhaps that is why I gave them grain last evening?

I hastened back into my house and quickly bundled up what few possessions I had that I wanted to take along, mostly my tools, and had them bundled onto old Jed by the time I saw Joseph and Mary come out their door with Yahushua. Joseph and I lashed their goods onto Jed, along with mine, while Mary got the little one situated on Delilah. I saw Ruth come up and nudge the baby with her nose, and I had the feeling she wanted to carry Yahushua herself. I made up my mind she would do so before the trip was over.

We were on the road and out of town long before anyone was up to see which way we went, or even that we had gone.

****

The years in Egypt were a mix of happy and hard. The gold given by the magi went a long way to provide for our stay. Both Joseph and I worked as much as we could, but being foreigners, work was scarce. It was a real treat, though, to see Yahushua growing up. He and Ruth bonded, and she followed him around like a puppy.

Joseph and Mary had begun a family together, and little James was a delight. I never saw a man so devoted to his family as was Joseph. On days we found work, he was always in a hurry to get home to them as soon as the evening came. On days we didn't have work away from home, he would build furniture for their house, but he ended up selling a good bit of it, making a nice side business.

Finally came the day Herod Antipas died. The angel appeared to Joseph again, telling him it was safe to return to Israel. Joseph didn't wake me in the middle of the night to tell me this time, though. Morning was soon enough for this trip.

Once we crossed back into Israel, we found out Archelaus ruled in his father's stead. With the angel's first warning echoing in his ears, Joseph was afraid to return to Bethlehem. We made our way instead to Nazareth, back to where it all started.

Joseph and Mary returned to their first home, on the back of Jacob's house, and got settled in right away, but I didn't return to my father's house for I got word my uncle had passed away childless, down in Bethphage, just a stone's throw east of Jerusalem, on the road to Bethany. Uncle Pharez left his home and property to me. With a sorrowful heart at leaving my close friends, I took Delilah and Ruth, but I left old Jed with Joseph. Jed was getting a bit old for working like we had worked him. He was still good to have around for light things, and I knew Joseph would care for him.

It didn't take me long to get settled into the house in Bethphage since I didn't have all that much as far as goods were concerned. We didn't bother to bring much with us from Egypt, so I got myself settled and found work at the temple again. I also was able to reacquaint myself with some cousins in Bethany, Lazarus and his sisters, Mary and Martha. Since my father had moved our family to Nazareth when I was still a child, we only saw them when we made our yearly trip to Jerusalem for Passover. I had not seen them at all during the time I was in Egypt.

One evening when I was at their home for supper, Martha introduced me to a young maiden, Deborah, and I was smitten! I had decided I was cut out to be a bachelor, not that I was all that old, but I just didn't see where getting married was worth all the fuss. My mind was changed instantly! Every chance I had, I was back at Lazarus' home hoping for another glimpse of Deborah, much to Martha's amusement. Martha did relent though, finally, and arranged the shidduch*, and she served as our chaperone. It didn't take me long to know for certain, and with her and Lazarus as character witnesses, I was able to make the agreement with Deborah's father, Eli, for her hand.

Because I had shared the home in Egypt with Joseph and Mary, I was able to lay aside some money, and since I had a house to bring her to, I had only to wait a year to marry Deborah and bring her home. I can honestly say marriage was the best thing that ever happened to me.

Because of all Joseph had taught me over the years, it was only a short time before I was promoted and made a supervisor of construction at the temple, and with Deborah caring for the house, we really did well.

Joseph, Mary, and their family always stopped by on their way to Jerusalem for Passover, giving us a chance to catch up on things and to see how their children were growing. Deborah and I were able to introduce our son Caleb to them the second year they stayed with us.

The year Yahushua turned twelve we had a real scare. Joseph and his family stopped by as usual on their way up to Passover, then Deborah, Caleb, our daughter Dinah, and I went up to the temple with them. We had quite a group as Lazarus, Mary, and Martha joined us, along with a number of others and their families. We laughed and sang from the Psalms, especially the Psalms of Ascents, the 120th through the 134th. These songs are often called Pilgrim Songs because of their association with going to Jerusalem. Generally, we just had a great time of fellowship that continued on through the Passover celebration and then the return trip. It seemed it always broke up when we got back to my house, which was not a full day's journey, but with all of the crowd and hustle and bustle, it was usually an all-day affair getting home after Passover. Joseph and Mary and their family would spend the night before they went on to Nazareth.

This year was different though. Joseph thought Mary knew where Yahushua was, and Mary thought Joseph knew. Both thought he was walking with friends in the group and didn't miss him until we reached home. Mary nearly went into a panic, but Joseph and I were able finally to calm her with the promise we would all go back to Jerusalem and find the lad. We left all of the children with Deborah and hastened back to the city, with Ruth carrying Mary, for she was with child again, and we needed to hurry.

Of course, we looked along the way, but no sign of Yahushua was to be found, nor had anyone seen him. We went back to the house in which we stayed while at the feast, but no one there had seen Yahushua either. Mary was nearly beside herself by now, and it was only by Joseph grabbing her by the arms and shaking her that he was able to get her attention enough to say we could not look for the boy in the dark. Besides that, he was old enough to care for himself: we would surely find him next day.

The next day we didn't find him, nor the day after that either, leaving Mary in a weeping heap upon her pallet when we went to bed at last that night. I don't believe she slept a wink but stayed awake crying and praying all night long. Finally, on the third day Mary said, "Let's try the temple. You know how he has always had a thing for the temple. I don't know why we didn't look there first."

This time instead of splitting up, we went looking together, and there he was, sitting on Solomon's Porch, with the scribes and chief rabbis asking him questions and discussing the Scriptures with him. They were amazed at the answers from such a young man.

Mary ran to Yahushua and threw her arms about him saying, "Son, why have you done this to us? We have searched for you weeping!"

Yahushua looked at his mother in astonishment. "Why did you look for me? Didn't you know I had to be about my father's business?"*

Everyone looked at him, puzzled, then looked at Joseph, shaking their heads. Yahushua obediently followed his mother as we left, and he returned home with us. Mary kept this in her heart and thought on it often, just as she did with the sayings of the shepherds and the magi so many years ago. The problem was that his birth, as spectacular as it had been, was twelve years past, and it was so easy to forget that Yahushua was "different."

****

For the next few years everything in their growing family seemed normal. Yahushua worked with Joseph, doing a good job from all accounts, but things changed when he was about thirty years of age. He began traveling about the countryside as an itinerate rabbi of sorts.

Soon after he began his new ministry, Yahushua, accompanied by some followers, escorted his mother to a wedding feast for some distant kin over in Cana. He and his mother had a good time getting reacquainted with folks they had not seen in some years.

On the fourth day of the feast, Mary overheard her cousin berating himself in the kitchen. It seems they had run short on wine. A lot more people had attended the festivities than had been planned for; in fact, quite a few had not even been invited! He was terribly embarrassed by the situation, but Mary told him not to worry. She would see what she could do for him, and she hurried out to find Yahushua.

"Son, I need your help. Elimelech has run short of wine."

"Woman,* my time has not yet come!"

Mary didn't waste time arguing with him but just smiled and walked away. She knew her son would not let her down. "Do what he tells you," she commanded the servants.

Yahushua shook his head in resignation and waved one of the servants over to him. "Those ceremonial water pots over there—yes, the big ones. Fill them with fresh water."

The servant looked up at Yahushua like he was mad, but he did as told, enlisting help from others, for those pots were at least twenty gallon pots, some of them thirty. Yahushua stood and waited for them to finish. "All the way to the brim," he called out once when it seemed they would quit.

When the pots were full and nearly overflowing, Yahushua nodded and said, "Thank you. Now, dip some out and offer it to the master of ceremonies."

The servant looked at Yahushua, fully believing he dealt with a lunatic, but the servant had no choice. If the master said something, the servant would blame it on Yahushua, though he knew he would probably be beaten. Shoulders hunched, he carried a pitcher of water to the emcee. I could see him speak softly, offering the water, and then he poured it into the wine cup and flinched as he stepped back.

The master of ceremonies took a sip and set the cup down before standing to his feet quickly and calling Elimelech. The poor servant trembled, awaiting the explosion he knew was coming.

"Elimelech, you crafty fellow! Most people put out good wine first and then start giving out the cheap stuff later, but you, you sly fellow, saved the best for last! Wonderful wine, my friend!"

The poor servant looked into his pitcher, puzzled, only to find wine. Yahushua did his best to make himself scarce. He didn't want anyone to know what had happened. Had I not seen it, I wouldn't have believed it either.

****

Over the next three years, I heard stories about Yahushua and his preaching. He really had the religious leaders in Jerusalem riled, but they could find nothing with which to fault him, though believe me, they tried! The scribes, Pharisees, and Sadducees did their best to trap him, but every time they tried to catch him with a question, he would turn it back on them with another question. It got to the point they offered a reward if anyone would come forward with something Yahushua had done so they could arrest him, but no one had anything for them.

The people, for the most part, followed him, telling stories of the miracles Yahushua did—feeding a tremendous crowd from one young lad's lunch, even stilling the waters on Gennesaret* during a tremendous storm by saying, "Peace. Be still." These stories, plus talk of blind men being made to see and lame men to walk, abounded. Even lepers had been healed.

The year after Yahushua turned water into wine, Joseph and Mary stopped on their way to Passover with the rest of their family. Joseph had his new jack along. Delilah was getting along in years now, so I asked Joseph about breeding Ruth with his jack. He was more than willing and wouldn't take anything for it.

"After all the times we used your donkeys? When did I ever pay you?"

I was willing to accept, but I still felt a little funny about it.

"Just don't name it after me!" was all Joseph would say, laughing. Mary didn't think he was funny at all.

****

Now the colt was born, a jack this time, and I decided to name him Jed after his grandsire. Old Jed had always been a faithful creature, and I could think of no better name for his progeny. Of course, it would be a while before I could start breaking him for use.

The next time I had a chance to see Yahushua, other than a passing hello at Temple during Passover, was at my cousin Lazarus' funeral.

Lazarus had come down with the fever, as so many of us do at times, but he didn't seem to be getting better. His sister,

Mary, sent a messenger to Yahushua, hoping that he would come and heal Lazarus as we had heard he had done with so many others—but he did not come and did not come. Finally, Lazarus died, and a mercy it was, many of us thought. He was so sick there at the last.

We buried him in a dugout tomb in the limestone rock of the hillside and sealed the doorway with a big stone before the day was out, as was our custom. After all, in this heat you don't wait around! The family all gathered, with the paid mourners doing their wailing and moaning. Not that they were needed! Mary and Martha were doing enough to satisfy the biggest funeral critic.

It was on the third day after—and I was getting rather tired of the whole ordeal—that we got word Yahushua was coming. Mary jumped up and ran out to meet him on the way. I didn't think she should be alone, so I went along with her. Otherwise I would not have heard what happened.

Mary, when she saw Yahushua, knelt down and wrapped her arms about his legs. "Lord*, if you had been here, my brother wouldn't have died!" She wept on Yahushua's feet, clearly exhausted from the stress of the last few days. "Even now I know God will give you whatever you ask for." She was begging.

Yahushua bent down and said gently, "Your brother will rise again."

"Oh, I know he will rise in the resurrection day."

Again, gently, Yahushua nearly whispered to her, "I am the resurrection and the life. He that believes in me, even though he is dead, shall live. And those that live and believe in me shall never die. Do you believe this?"

"Yes, Lord; I believe you are the Mashiach, the Son of God, which should come into the world." She rose and walked back to the house, where she whispered to Martha, "The Master is come."

Martha jumped to her feet and came out to meet us. The mourners, thinking she was going to the grave to weep, followed. When she came to Yahushua, she did as her sister had done and fell at his feet, saying, "If you would have been here, my brother wouldn't have died."

Yahushua saw her tears and all of the mourners following her, and it troubled him.

"Where have you laid him?" he asked quietly, and then he, too, broke down and wept.

The mourners, most of whom knew Yahushua and Lazarus and knew how close they were, nodded to each other and said, "Look how much he loved him." But some of the mourners—there being a critic in every crowd said, "He healed blind men. If he would have come, could he not have saved him?"

Yahushua groaned quietly in his grief as he came to the grave and then said, "Take away the stone."

Martha quickly said, "But Lord, it's been four days! By now he stinks!"

"Didn't I tell you if you would only believe you would see the glory of God?"

They rolled away the stone, and Yahushua raised his eyes toward Heaven and prayed, "Father, I'm glad that you have heard me and that you always hear me, but because of all of these that stand by, I said it that they might hear and believe that you sent me." Then Yahushua with a shout said, "Lazarus, come out!"

Everyone stared open-mouthed at Yahushua. But they all were more amazed when Lazarus came hobbling out of the grave with his body and feet bound in grave clothes and a napkin wrapped around his face.

"Loose him, and let him go!"

Oh, but there was an excited crowd around that day! Yahushua went with Lazarus and his sisters to their home to celebrate, and the rest of the crowd scattered to tell the story everywhere. The religious leaders in Jerusalem were incensed, and they plotted how to kill Lazarus to keep the story from spreading—and how to kill Yahushua, too.

****

I had been working with the new Jed for a few weeks when I got word Yahushua was at Mary and Martha's house with Lazarus. Just six days before the Passover, when all of the festivities were going on and the women were working feverishly to have their houses prepared, Deborah and I were invited over for dinner. Martha prepared and served the dinner, and she was quite peeved at Mary because Mary kept sitting at Yahushua's feet, listening to him teach. Martha fussed to Yahushua once about Mary just sitting there, but he would have nothing to do with it.

Next day, as I was busy about the stable, two men walked up to where I had Ruth and Jed tied out at the fence, and they started to untie Jed's rope.

"Hey, what do you think you are doing? That's my donkey!"

"The Master has need of him," one of them said. It was then I recognized Simon.

"Oh. Go in peace!" I watched as they led young Jed and Ruth out to the main road from Bethany, past our house in Bethphage. I saw Simon lead Jed up to Yahushua. He and John had laid their cloaks over Jed's back. Ruth nuzzled Yahushua a time or two, and I was afraid what Jed would do. But, when Yahushua sat on him, Jed just walked, head high, as if he had done it every day of his life.

J.L. Callison

Quite a crowd gathered along the road that day, cutting down palm fronds and throwing them in the road, some even taking off their cloaks and laying them in the way so my donkey wouldn't get his hooves dusty.

"Hosanna! Blessed is the King of Israel that comes in the name of the Lord!"

I thought about it later and remembered what the prophet Zechariah had said about the Mashiach riding into Jerusalem on the foal of an ass.

****

It was quite a week, with a large crowd gathered in the city for Passover, many of them there because they knew Yahushua would be in the city, and they wanted to see him.

Of course the religious leaders were doing all they could to quell the joy of the people.

Mary came up early, and we had a good time catching up on things, although it was bittersweet. Joseph had died during the winter, leaving her alone—most of her children being grown.

Mid-week, things got ugly in a hurry. The word I got later was that the priests had found some men who would give testimony against Yahushua, accusing him of breaking Moses' laws. The priests went to the Roman governor and asked for troops. One of Jesus' disciples had agreed to sell him out and led the troops and priests to a garden where Yahushua liked to pray when in town. They captured him there—although "captured" is really too strong of a word because Yahushua put up no fight. He even told Simon to sheathe his sword when he tried to come to Yahushua's defense.

The religious leaders took Yahushua illegally before the Sanhedrin late at night, then went over to Herod and got him up. Herod refused to hear them, saying, "Take it to Pontus

Pilate," which they did early the next morning. They raised such a ruckus that Pilate finally allowed them to take Yahushua out and crucify him, caving to their wishes only after the religious leaders threatened to tell Caesar that Pilate was soft on traitors.

Mary was beside herself with grief at our home. She wanted to be with her son, so Deborah and I went with her.

We followed along as they led Yahushua and two others out of the city, through the gate in the wall to the crossroads outside of town, the place they call "the place of the skull" because that is where David buried Goliath's head. There they crucified him. Yahushua's beard had been torn from his face, and he had been beaten so badly one would not recognize him as a man if it wasn't known that he was.

The whole process was strange. The two murderous thieves that were crucified that day had as many as sixteen tough legionaires holding them down to nail them to the cross, but when they came to Yahushua, it only took two. He truly laid his life down! No one took it from him.

****

When it was all over, Joseph of Arimathæa, who up to this point had been a secret disciple of Yahushua, begged Pilate for the body so that he could be buried before the time of preparation for the Passover. Pilate agreed, and since I had Ruth there for Mary to ride, we used her to carry Yahushua's body to Joseph's own tomb.

****

The disciples, along with Mary and the other women, gathered together in the same upper room where Jesus had celebrated the Passover with them. Deborah and I joined them. To say the atmosphere was gloomy doesn't begin to touch it.

29

Because the High Sabbath of the Passover was followed by the regular Shabbat, none of us ventured from the room, other than for necessities. We mourned together, leaning on each other for support and encouragement.

The disciples in particular were torn as to what they were going to do now. After all, without the Mashiach to follow, what were their options? Go back to their fishing boats or other occupations? Levi, or Matthew, as he frequently is called, could hardly go back to being a publican, could he?

The night following the Sabbath was even more troubled than the nights preceding. A rumor the Sanhedrin sought those of us who followed the master—that our very lives were in danger—was going around.

Very early the next morning, just before sunrise, my wife Deborah left with Mary Magdela, James' mother Mary, Joanna, Salome, and other of the women who went to anoint the body of Yahushua. Because of the preparation for the Passover, there had not been time after he was crucified, but it was a job that had to be done. I know none of them looked forward to the task. After all, it had been three days already, and even in a hewn tomb, it could not be pleasant. Then, too, they didn't know how they could get the stone rolled from the door, for it was quite heavy.

Needless to say, when they got to the garden and found the tomb opened, they were amazed and fearful. Mary Magdela ran back to the upper room and told Peter and John, who ran with her to the tomb to see what happened. The other women had gone into the tomb and found it empty, but when they went to step back out, as Deborah told me later, two men with white clothing that glowed like lightning asked them, "Why do you seek the living among the dead? He is not here; he has risen! Remember how he told you, while he was still with you in

Galilee: 'The Son of Man must be delivered over to the hands of sinners, be crucified and on the third day be raised again.'"

The women fled just before John arrived and looked in the door. He, much younger than Peter, had outrun him by quite a bit. Peter, huffing and puffing, pushed John out of the way so that he could enter the tomb. He and John saw the grave clothes lying there, empty. Mary Magdela came up behind them, and when they left, she looked in.

She told me what happened later, "I looked inside, and there on the bench where we had laid the body, two angels asked me, 'Why are you crying?' I said, 'Because they have taken my Lord away, and I don't know where they have laid him.' I heard a noise behind me and turned. A man stood there—one of the gardeners, I thought."

"'Why are you crying? Who are you looking for?' he asked, and he was ever so kind. 'Sir, if you carried him away, please tell me where so I can tend to him.'"

Mary looked at me with the sweetest smile. "The man said, 'Mary.' It was Yahushua!"

Can you imagine the tumult in the room that day? We talked, and we talked. We argued, and we discussed. One does not just rise from the dead. Sure, we had seen Yahushua raise a couple of people, or at least some of us had. But one does not raise oneself, does one?

Mid-afternoon, Cleopas and one of the others—I can't recall his name—left us for their homes in Emmaus. Thomas—or in Greek, Didymus, it means twin—also left. Where he went, nobody knows. Of the whole group in the room, he was the most doubtful of the news that Peter, John, and Mary Magdela told us.

We barred the door because the rumors still went round, and we talked some more. If there is anything this group can do, it is talk!

Supper was just over, and we were ready to douse the lights and sleep when there was a pounding at the door. Cleopas and the other disciple—why can't I remember his name—were there, chests heaving for breath. They had run all of the way from Emmaus with the news.

"Yahushuah lives! He walked with us on the road and talked with us from the Scriptures about the Mashiach and about how he had to be put to death and rise again. Oh, how blind we have been! Remember what Esaius said? 'He would be punished by God?' 'He would be pierced for our transgressions?' 'The LORD makes his life an offering for our sin?' And how David wrote in the twenty second psalm? John—you were right there when he died. Isn't it true he cried out and asked God why He forsook him? See? It is as it was written."

We were all gathered around the two when we sensed a presence behind us. The doors were bolted, but Yahushua stood there. Some of us thought it was his ghost. He asked us for a piece of fish and ate it before us to assure us he was real. Then, he showed us his hands and side, where they had been pierced.

****

One morning, just a few weeks later, I awoke, knowing somehow that the day was going to be special. Deborah and I were going to go into Jerusalem to see Yahushuah. I led Ruth from the kraal for Deborah. Since she and the Master had had a special relationship ever since she was but a foal, I wanted to take her.

It is almost as if Yahushua and his followers waited for us, for we had no more than reached the house with the upper room when the group came out. Mary and the Master walked over to Ruth together, and Ruth nuzzled him, knowingly. John helped Mary onto Ruth, and the Master led the way out of the city to Bethany, speaking to us of what we needed to do now.

We came to an open space, and he stopped and blessed us. Then, while we watched, he ascended into the clouds.

We stood dumbfounded, staring, until two men in white clothing appeared and asked why we looked into the heavens. "This same Yahushua will come again, just as you saw him go."

As if they spoke to her, Ruth bobbed her head, turned, and led us back into Jerusalem. I glanced into the face of the woman riding the burro. She is exhausted by the events of the last two months. My wife walks alongside, to assist if needed.

I can't wait for Yahushua to return!

****

Of course, you know the story, and how it all happened. I wanted you to know how my donkeys served the Master.

Glossary

1. Ben (or Bar). Means "son of." A young lady would have the word "Bat" in her formal name, which means "daughter of."

2. Ketubah. A written contract specifying the dowry the young man was paying for the daughter, the time, place, size, and arrangements of the wedding, and all of the terms of maintenance of the marriage.

3. Shiddukhin ceremony. The engagement or espousal ceremony. This was a binding arrangement that could only be broken by a bill of divorcement. It meant two people were as committed to each other as married people could be. The only thing lacking in the marriage was the formal "chuppah" ceremony and their physical union. "Chuppah" is pronounced with a guttural "H" for the "Ch".

4. Shekel. A shekel equals 10.52 grams of silver, approximately \$7.35 at the time of this writing.

5. Mite (or lepton). The smallest coin struck. It was bronze. It equaled approximately 1/128th of a day's wage for an unskilled laborer, about .0026 Shekels.

6. Jenny. A female donkey. A male donkey is called a jack. A donkey was frequently called an ass.

7. Mashiach. Messiah, the anointed one. In the New Testament (Greek), Christos, Christ.

8. Aleichim Shalom. "Upon you be peace." Normally the response to a greeting, but in this case an expression of the wish for peace of mind and heart.

9. Khan. Inn.

10. Publican. A tax collector. Usually a Jewish man working for the Roman government for a commission on the taxes collected. They set the fees themselves and were commonly known to be crooked and unfair in their dealings.

11. Shabbat. Sabbath.

12. Shidduch. A match-making arrangement introducing prospective marriage partners and families. Sometimes, the bride and groom would not actually meet until the Shiddukhin when they signed the Ketubah, unlike in this story.

13. "Didn't you know I had to be about my father's business?" - Yahushua, at age 12, would be beginning an apprenticeship, normally with his father, hence his question. The onlookers were confused because they believed Joseph to be Yahushua's father, not God.

14. "Woman, my time has not yet come." For Yahushua to address his mother as "Woman" was not rude, nor was it in poor taste. It was a common form of address in the Hebrew idiom. It's very similar to saying, "Ma'am", but more personal.

15. Gennesaret. The Sea of Galilee.

16. Lord. Adonai – Lord or Master. Much like we would say "Sir" now. Mary did not call him "Lord" as a reference to deity.

About J.L. Callison

J.L. Callison was an early reader, whose third-grade teacher encouraged his love of reading. He read over 300 books that year, and was reading on an eighth grade level by year's end. He developed a wide range of reading interests, and read volumes A-H of the World Book Encyclopedia! He loves to collect books, and has well over a thousand books in his library, many of which he has read more than once. Young adult is his favorite genre, for as he says, he refuses to grow up.

He studied for the ministry, and has served in lay capacities for much of his adult life, but always with a youth ministry focus. He has been, along with his wife, a junior-high youth sponsor and teacher for most of the last twenty-five years. He also served in rescue mission and jail ministries for several years.

He and his wife of 39 years live in Illinois. They have five grown children and are blessed with five grandchildren.

Other Titles by J.L. Callison

Stranded at Romson's Lodge is an action/adventure story of two teens, kidnapped and flown to remote upstate Maine and dropped off at a hunting lodge. Their kidnapper hits a goose on takeoff and crashes, leaving them *Stranded at Romson's Lodge*. With thirty-five miles between them and the nearest hunting lodge, Jed knows it is up to him to care for a homesick city girl until someone finds them. Is he up to the task? This was going to be interesting. Not only did he have to babysit a tenderfoot, he had to listen to her, too.

Elizabeth, a city girl, has never been away from home, especially out in the wilderness with no amenities. Can she learn to cook on a wood stove or over an open fire? And what about wild animals? Wolves? Bears? Coyotes?

Connect With J.L. Callison

I love to hear from my readers and appreciate any feedback or reviews given. Please feel free to connect with me through email at jl@jlcallison.com, through my website, www.jlcallison.com or on Facebook at https://www.facebook.com/J.L.Callison/?ref=aymt_homepage _panel

I make every attempt to reply to communications promptly.

If you are interested in a speaker for any size group I am happy to oblige. Please connect through my email and I will make every effort to meet your needs.

www.ingramcontent.com/pod-product-compliance
Lightning Source LLC
Chambersburg PA
CBHW070652130626
46555CB00006B/2839